Jasper is out of control!

"Is this your lunch?" Jasper asked, grabbing Louise's lunch box.

"Hands off!" said Louise.

"Now, now," said Jasper. "Is that any way to act after a whole summer apart?" He opened the lid. "What do we have here? Hmmm . . . sandwich, chips, cookies."

"Cut it out," said Louise. What was wrong with Jasper? He had never done anything like this before.

"I missed breakfast this morning," Jasper continued. "Did you know it's the most important meal of the day? Now that I'm bigger, I have to pay attention to these things."

He shoved the cookies into his mouth.

Accident Branch
Ruth Enlow Library
P.O. Box 154
Accident, MD 21520

OTHER CHAPTER BOOKS FROM PUFFIN

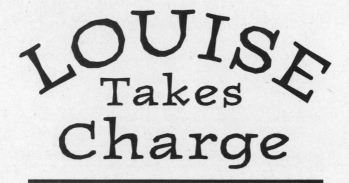

LOUISE Takes Charge

by STEPHEN KRENSKY
pictures by SUSANNA NATTI

PUFFIN BOOKS

For Ashley and Laura,
who like to take charge too
S.K.

To Mary, Catrine, Ronnie, and Ellen,
my take-charge buddies
S.N.

01018 5352

PUFFIN BOOKS
Published by the Penguin Group
Penguin Putnam Books for Young Readers,
345 Hudson Street, New York, New York 10014, U.S.A.
Penguin Books Ltd, 27 Wrights Lane, London W8 5TZ, England
Penguin Books Australia Ltd, Ringwood, Victoria, Australia
Penguin Books Canada Ltd, 10 Alcorn Avenue, Toronto, Ontario, Canada M4V 3B2
Penguin Books (N.Z.) Ltd, 182-190 Wairau Road, Auckland 10, New Zealand

Penguin Books Ltd, Registered Offices: Harmondsworth, Middlesex, England

First published in the United States of America by Dial Books for Young Readers,
a member of Penguin Putnam Inc., 1998
Published by Puffin Books,
a division of Penguin Putnam Books for Young Readers, 2000

1 3 5 7 9 10 8 6 4 2

Text copyright © Stephen Krensky, 1998
Illustrations copyright © Susanna Natti, 1998
All rights reserved

THE LIBRARY OF CONGRESS HAS CATALOGED THE DIAL EDITION AS FOLLOWS:
Louise takes charge/by Stephen Krensky; pictures by Susanna Natti.
—1st ed.
p. cm.
Summary: Louise enlists the aid of everyone in her class and
together they outwit Jasper the bully.
ISBN 0-8037-2305-9 (trade).—ISBN 0-8037-2306-7 (lib.)
[1. Bullies—Fiction. 2. Schools—Fiction.] I. Natti, Susanna, ill
II. Title.
PZ7.K883Lo 1998 [Fic]—dc21 97-37441 CIP AC

Puffin Books ISBN 0-14-130822-2

Printed in the United States of America

Except in the United States of America, this book is sold subject to the condition that
it shall not, by way of trade or otherwise, be lent, re-sold, hired out, or otherwise
circulated without the publisher's prior consent in any form of binding or cover
other than that in which it is published and without a similar condition
including this condition being imposed on the subsequent purchaser.

RL: 2.4

003438 A

CHAPTER 1

"Come on, Louise!" her mother said firmly. "You don't have much time."

It was the first day of school, and Louise Page was not happy. Things were already going too fast. Her brain was still set to a summer schedule of bare feet and lazy mornings. Tuning in to the real world was not easy.

Her brother waved his hand in front of her face. "Earth to Louise. . . . Come in, Louise."

"Cut it out, Lionel."

He inspected her cereal bowl. "You'd better eat fast. Your cereal is getting old."

Louise took a spoonful. "Cereal doesn't get

RUTH ENLOW LIBRARY OF GARRETT CO.

old, Lionel. It gets soggy or limp." She paused. "Or sometimes mushy."

Lionel shrugged. "Mine gets old," he said, carrying his bowl to the sink.

Their father came in from the living room. "Ah, the first day of school," he said. Mr. Page was wearing his favorite tie—the one with the exploding fireworks—in honor of the occasion. "New classes, new friendships . . ."

"New homework!" Louise and Lionel groaned together.

"True," said Mr. Page. "But you kids have it easy. When I was your age—"

"No time for ancient history now," said Louise, glancing at the clock. "We'll miss the bus."

"Ancient history?" said her father. "I don't think so. These are classic stories. Timeless. You're lucky to hear them."

"Can we be lucky later?" asked Lionel, grabbing his jacket.

"I suppose so."

Louise gave her father a kiss good-bye. And then before he could change his mind, she followed Lionel out the door.

Louise's new classroom was just down the hall from the one she had been in the year before. After a whole summer, though, her memories of last year's class seemed very far away. It felt like she had read about them in a book instead of actually living them herself.

The chairs and desks sat neatly in rows, gleaming like freshly scrubbed faces. Louise took a deep breath. The air smelled a little funny, she thought—a mixture of plaster dust and detergent.

The room began to fill up. Louise had seen some of the kids, like Emily and Megan, a lot over the summer. Megan, in fact, would probably know exactly how many days they had spent together. She kept track of things like that. Louise had seen the others a little around town.

Her thoughts were interrupted as a large shadow passed over her. Goose bumps appeared on her arms as she turned quickly, and found herself facing Jasper Hall.

Louise remembered Jasper plainly enough. He tried way too hard to be popular, always laughing loudest at his own jokes and paying himself compliments before anyone else had a chance. Louise had just rolled her eyes and ignored him when he got too far out of line.

There was no ignoring him now. Jasper must have grown five inches since June.

"Hello, Jasper," she said. "Did you have a good summer?"

Jasper grunted. "I had a big summer," he declared. His muscles expanded as he talked, like balloons being inflated.

"So I see." Not everything about Jasper had changed. His hair still stuck up in the back, and he still had that gap between his front teeth.

"Is this your lunch?" Jasper asked, grabbing Louise's lunch box.

"Hands off!" said Louise.

"Now, now," said Jasper. "Is that any way to act after a whole summer apart?" He opened the lid. "What do we have here? Hmmm . . . sandwich, chips, cookies."

"Cut it out," said Louise. What was wrong with Jasper? He had never done anything like this before.

"I missed breakfast this morning," Jasper continued. "Did you know it's the most important meal of the day? Now that I'm bigger, I have to pay attention to these things."

He shoved the cookies into his mouth.

Louise looked around. Unfortunately their teacher, Mr. Hathaway, was still busy in the hall.

"Are you finished?" said Louise.

Jasper tossed the lunch box back to her. "For now. Unless you want to make something of it."

He made a fist the size of a basketball.

Louise hesitated. She wanted to take that fist and stuff it into the nearest trash can. But she also wanted to live long enough to see her next birthday.

Ringgggg.

"Saved by the bell," sneered Jasper. He smiled.

It was not a pretty sight.

CHAPTER 2

Louise tried to push Jasper out of her mind so she could listen to Mr. Hathaway. But Jasper's creepy smile kept distracting her.

"Are you okay?" whispered Emily, who was sitting beside her. "You're fidgeting a lot."

Louise blinked. "I'll tell you later," she said, and looked back at Mr. Hathaway, who was outlining the joys of simple fractions.

It was not until recess that Louise finally got a chance to tell Emily what had happened with Jasper.

Emily's mouth made a big O. "What a slug!" she fumed. "Who does he think he is, King Kong?"

Louise was about to answer when they were both distracted by raised voices from the baseball field.

"We've already picked captains," said Brendan. "I'm one. Lauren is the other."

He was speaking to Jasper. A crowd of kids had gathered around them. Louise and Emily watched to see what would happen.

"Is that so?" said Jasper. He walked over and stood on Brendan's foot.

"Mind if I take your place?" he asked.

Brendan squirmed, but he couldn't get free. He pushed at Jasper. It had no effect. Jasper didn't even bother to push back. He just stood there with his arms crossed.

"Well?" he said.

Brendan's freckles stuck out a little as he turned redder. "I—I guess not."

"Good." Jasper lifted his foot. "I knew we could work this out." He turned to Lauren. "I'll take first pick."

"We should buck up," said Lauren, putting one hand behind her back.

"Let's not waste time," said Jasper. "Recess is so short. Besides, I want to go first." He stared hard at Lauren's feet. "Any problem with that?"

Lauren looked at Brendan, who was standing on one foot. "All right, all right."

"Good. Tell you what, though. Your side can be up first."

After all the picks were made, Jasper called his team together for an announcement.

"I'm going to pitch," he said.

Jasper had always played catcher before, but that was the old Jasper, the small Jasper. The new super-size Jasper had other ideas.

"I usually pitch," said Stephanie. "Have you had any practice?"

"Over the summer," said Jasper. "You can take my old position."

Stephanie stomped off behind home plate. The rest of the team took their places.

"Batter up!" said Jasper.

The game started. Jasper may have practiced over the summer, but he still needed some work. His first pitch was in the dirt. His second sailed over Danny's head. The pitches didn't get much better after that.

Nobody on Lauren's team wanted to swing at all.

"You guys are too picky," said Jasper. "You're holding up the game. I don't like that. Understand?"

They understood. As Louise and Emily watched from the sidelines, the batters started swinging at everything. They swung at high pitches like lumberjacks chopping wood. They swung at low pitches like golfers teeing off.

Almost all of them struck out.

When the bell rang, Jasper's team was ahead 7–0.

"We won!" shouted Jasper. "A shutout too."

Lauren snorted. "Only because everyone swung at your crummy pitches."

"It's a free country," said Jasper. Then he laughed and walked away.

CHAPTER 3

Louise hoped that Jasper was just having a bad first day. Maybe he had gotten up on the wrong side of the bed. Or maybe he was grouchy from staying up too late.

But the next day was no better. In fact, the whole next week was a nightmare. Jasper kept getting bolder and bolder. On the following Monday Louise overheard him talking to Kristina and Tim after Mr. Hathaway had put them in groups to start a unit on Ancient Egypt.

"I'm so glad we'll be working together on this new project," Jasper said.

"There's a lot to do," said Kristina. "We

have to find out all about the Great Pyramid. We'll need books from the library."

"Good point," said Jasper. "I think you should do that."

"And we're going to need stuff from the art store too," Tim reminded them.

"Another good point," said Jasper. "Why don't you handle that?"

"And then we'll have to do the research and make the pictures."

Jasper nodded. "You know, that part's a lot of work. It wouldn't be fair for either of you to do it alone. You should work together."

Kristina frowned. "Jasper, you keep telling us what we're going to do. What are *you* going to do?"

Jasper leaned back in his chair. "Me?" he said, smiling. "I'm going to find out more about the pharaohs. They really knew how to boss people around. There's a lot to be learned from them."

At lunch the teachers on duty were so busy

with the usual uproar, they didn't notice Jasper moving around.

He sat down next to Elizabeth as she carefully unwrapped a cupcake.

"That looks good," he said.

"I saved it from my brother Jonathan's birthday party."

Jasper looked shocked. "Jonathan had a party—and he didn't invite me."

"Jasper, you don't even know Jonathan."

"That makes no difference. I still feel bad. But I know what would make me feel better."

He grabbed the cupcake and stuffed it into his mouth.

"Hey!" Elizabeth shouted.

"Tasty," mumbled Jasper. "Tell Jonathan I approved."

Chris was next.

"Tuna subs are okay," Jasper told him, taking half for himself. "But leave out the pickles next time. I don't like them."

Megan was sitting across the table. There was no food in front of her, but her closed mouth was moving a little.

"What are you eating?" Jasper asked her.

Megan swallowed. "Nothing," she said. "The chance of my eating something was only 7%."

Megan was very big on statistics.

"Well, let's take a look at that 7%."

Megan sighed and handed over the bag of potato chips.

"That's better," said Jasper. "Don't hold out on your friends."

When Jasper reached Louise, he frowned.

"Hellll-o, Jasper," she said. "Fancy meeting you here."

"I'm here every day," said Jasper.

"So you are," agreed Louise.

"Yeah, yeah," said Jasper. "Just tell me what's on today's menu."

Louise held up her sandwich. "Help yourself."

Jasper took a sniff. "That's disgusting! What's in it?"

"Let's see." Louise lifted the bread. "There's spinach. . . . And I think American cheese. . . . Oh, and let's not forget the liver."

"Gross. What's wrong with you, anyway?"

Louise looked surprised. "What do you mean?" she asked.

"I mean the stuff you're eating. Today it's liver and whatever. Friday it was peanut butter and onions. The day before it was some dumb tuna-and-tofu combo."

"My mother likes to mix as many of the food groups together as possible. She thinks it saves time."

"I don't care why you're eating it," said Jasper. "I just want you to stop with this baloney."

"Liver," Louise reminded him.

"Don't get smart with me, Louise. I want regular food."

"Sorry," said Louise. "You know how difficult parents can be." She took a small bite. "But I'm happy to share."

"That's what you always say," Jasper growled. He got up abruptly and continued his rounds.

As soon as Jasper walked away, Louise spat the sandwich bite into a napkin.

"Yuck!" she muttered.

Emily giggled beside her. "Not too good, huh?"

"I'll say. These sandwiches were the only things I could think of making that The Bottomless Pit wouldn't like."

"At least you stopped him."

"True," said Louise. She took out her real sandwich from inside a hollowed-out book. "But there has to be a better way. If I have to keep making these disgusting things, I may lose my appetite for good."

CHAPTER 4

That night Louise lay on her bed, thinking. She was in a rotten mood. Just after school Jasper had made her do his math homework. He said it was to make up for her stupid lunches.

She felt a little better knowing that she had done some of the harder problems wrong on purpose, but that wasn't enough.

Louise punched her pillow. She had to think of something. Jasper was too big and too mean for any physical stuff. There had to be another way to stop him.

"Knock, knock."

Her father stood in the doorway. "I'm just

checking in on you," he said. "On page 34 of *The Father's Handbook* it states quite clearly that I'm supposed to ask questions if you seem troubled."

"Is it that obvious?" Louise asked.

"Uh-huh." He smiled at her. "During dinner Lionel said a number of things that usually would have prompted a comment or two from you. But you were as silent as the sphinx."

Louise smiled weakly. "That reminds me. I have to write up my report about the pharaoh Cheops and all the people he conquered." She sighed. "Is it really true what they say about 'brains over brawn'?"

Her father paused. "The people with brains all like to think so."

"I mean, Cheops got to do pretty much whatever he wanted just because he had such a big army. Do you think someone could have outsmarted him without the same strength?"

Mr. Page considered it. "We're only talking about Ancient Egypt, right? Hmmm . . . Well, one person alone couldn't oppose a pharaoh. But if one person could convince other people to oppose the pharaoh, they might make a change. It's like that saying that there's strength in numbers. Who knows how much strength they could create together?"

Louise nodded. "I guess teamwork makes a difference."

"Anything else?"

"Not yet. But, thanks."

Her father ruffled her hair and started for the door. "Just remember, eventually the pharaohs were defeated. They lost their power when they got too greedy."

Louise rolled over on her bed. Jasper was as greedy as any pharaoh, but how far would he try to go?

"Beware, villain!"

Louise rolled her eyes. "Not now, Lionel," she said. "I'm not in the mood."

Her younger brother had entered her room wearing a knight's helmet. He was holding a cardboard sword and a shield. They were

both covered with aluminum foil.

"Villains are never in the mood," Lionel said. "It does not matter. I will serve you no longer."

"What are you talking about?"

"It will do no good to play the fool—though you play it well. For five years I have been your loyal apprentice. You promised me my own horse and armor at the end of that time. But you have broken your word."

Louise sighed. "So I'm in trouble, right?"

Lionel raised his sword defiantly. "You may jest if you like. But you are also doomed. I served you faithfully. Now I give you fair warning. When next we meet, it will be on the field of battle. Then there will be a reckoning between us."

Louise threw a pillow at the doorway, but Lionel was already gone.

"Knights," she muttered. "Apprentices, indeed."

Suddenly she smiled. An apprentice was a helper, someone who served a master and learned from him. Someone to do his dirty work. Someone who was under his protection.

Louise let out a deep breath. It wouldn't be easy, but she now knew what to do.

CHAPTER 5

The next morning Louise told Emily and Megan about her plan before the bell rang. During recess they told Andrew and Peter, who spread the news to Sean and K.C. By the end of lunch everyone knew that something was up.

Everyone but Jasper. Louise had made it very clear that Jasper must not know about anything.

The plan started with a secret meeting after school. Nobody had ever called for such a meeting before. It sounded very mysterious.

Everyone who could get there met under a tree in the playground.

"You probably can guess why I asked you here," Louise began.

"Jasper, I'll bet," said Christine. She rubbed her shoulder where Jasper had bumped it as he rounded first base.

Everyone looked around nervously.

"Do you think it's safe?"

"He seems to be everywhere."

"I check under my bed before I go to sleep," said Joey. "And even when I don't find him, I keep expecting him to walk in demanding my pillow and half the blanket."

"Don't worry," said Louise. "I heard him mention watching his older brother's baseball game. We'll have all the time we need."

"Time for what?" asked Matthew.

"To talk," said Louise. "We can't let Jasper boss us around forever."

The others nodded.

Jacqueline made a face. "At lunch today he said he was going to share. Then he took a bite from each of my cookies. I could have the rest, he told me." She shuddered.

"Yesterday," said Emily, "he made me carry him piggyback over a puddle. If I hadn't been wearing new pants, I would have pitched him over."

Megan blinked. "If you had, the chances he would have killed you are—" she paused, "98%."

"I know." Emily sighed. "But I would have died with a smile on my face."

"Look," said Louise, "it's been hard on us all. Mr. Hathaway does his best, but he can't be everywhere at once. Even if he could be, we'd still have to worry about after school and weekends. That's why we have to work together."

Alex was doodling in the dirt. A giant monster was attacking some innocent villagers. The monster was throwing them around like toys.

"What kind of action?" he asked. "I've tried standing up to Jasper. It doesn't help. He just stands a little taller and stomps on our feet."

"I know, I know," said Louise. "We've tried to stop him by ourselves. Maybe that's the trouble. We need to work as a team. Jasper may be big, but he's not bigger than all of us put together."

"Close, though," muttered Julia.

Everybody laughed.

"All right," said Louise, "let's not give up before we've even started. Now listen carefully. I have a plan."

Everyone huddled in a circle. Louise had to explain things twice to get rid of any confusion.

"It sounds tricky."

"What if he gets suspicious?"

"Pretending makes me nervous."

"I know it's complicated," said Louise. "But we'll only go forward step-by-step. Of course, if anyone has a better idea, feel free to speak up."

Nobody did.

"Okay, then." Louise folded her arms. "Remember, the plan won't work if anyone blabs.

Think of this as a class project, the biggest one any class has ever tried."

"Do you really think it will work?" asked Megan. "I calculate our chances of success to be only 23%."

"In that case," said Louise, "we'll just have to beat the odds."

CHAPTER 6

The next day Louise got to school early. Besides her books and lunch she had brought a bottle of spray cleaner, a scraper, and some rags. She used these cleaning supplies to wash Jasper's desk and chair.

When Jasper arrived, Louise greeted him warmly. "Good morning," she said. "I hope you approve."

Jasper frowned. "Approve? Approve of what?"

"Well, I came in a little early and worked on your desk."

Jasper looked. His desk was shinier. He knelt down and inspected underneath. All of

his old gum wads were gone.

"Where's the booby trap?" he asked.

Louise laughed. "Booby trap? There's no booby trap."

Jasper was not convinced. He dropped a book on the seat to see if the chair would collapse. It didn't.

"Really, you're perfectly safe," Louise assured him. "If I had booby-trapped your desk, would I stand around waiting for you to catch me?"

Jasper had to admit that would be kind of stupid.

"Anyway, that's not all I have to tell you." Louise patted her lunch box. "I brought you a roast beef sandwich today."

"With artichoke dressing, I bet."

"Nope."

"Is there broccoli loaf mixed in?"

"Nope."

Jasper sneered. "Is it poisoned?"

Louise shook her head. "You've been watching too many horror movies. Naturally, I've got chips too."

Jasper scratched his head. "What happened to your mother mixing all those food groups together?"

"Oh, she read an article that changed her mind. Turns out it hurts your digestion. Your stomach gets confused or something."

"I can believe that," Jasper muttered.

Louise opened her notebook. "Also, I have some ideas that should help you understand fractions better."

Jasper stepped back. "You're not the real Louise, are you? You're an alien that's taken over her body."

"No, no, I'm the real Louise." She motioned Jasper closer. "It's just that I've been thinking about all the things you've accomplished since school started. You've really taken charge here."

Jasper puffed out his chest. "I have, haven't I?"

"Everyone does what you say."

"True."

"Everyone's afraid of you."

"True again."

Louise folded her arms. "I mean, when it comes to having your own way, you've done everything one person could do."

Jasper grinned. "I suppose you're right."

"But . . . " said Louise.

Jasper's smile faded.

"But what?"

"Nothing."

"Tell me, Louise."

"It's nothing. Really."

Jasper frowned. "Come on, Louise. You know you'll tell me in the end."

"All right, all right. You see, as good as you are, one person can only do so much."

Jasper shrugged. "So? I can't be more than one person."

"I know. But you could have help."

"Help? What kind of help?"

"An apprentice," said Louise.

"A *what?*"

"An apprentice. Someone to keep track of things. An assistant to do your bidding."

Jasper rubbed his chin. "Is this apprentice a kind of servant?"

"Yes."

"Gee, I'd probably be the only kid in town with an apprentice." He paused. "Wait a minute! I know what you're up to.

"You do?" A chill swept through Louise.

"I'm not stupid. You're telling me all this because you want to be my apprentice."

Louise blushed. "It's that obvious, is it?"

"I can usually tell about people," Jasper said. "It's like a sixth sense with me."

"I can see that. So, can I have the job?"

Jasper was thinking. "Do I have to pay you?"

"No, no. As an apprentice, learning from

you is my only reward."

"Sounds fair," said Jasper. "Okay, the job's yours."

"Thank you," said Louise. "I know I'll never regret this."

CHAPTER 7

Louise began her new job at recess.

"I'll take that," she said to Jasper as they headed outside.

"Take what?" said Jasper.

"Your baseball glove."

"Why?"

"You shouldn't have to carry it," Louise explained. "That's what I'm here for."

"Really?"

Louise nodded. "An apprentice has many duties," she said.

Jasper smiled. "This is better than I expected."

Out on the field, Jasper and Megan picked

for teams. "Hurry up," said Jasper while Megan debated her choices.

"Easy for you to say," sniffed Megan. "You picked first. That increased your chances of winning by 17%."

"Just get on with it."

Megan finally made her picks and the teams took the field. When Jasper came up to bat, Louise cheered him on.

"What's going on, Louise?"

"Are you crazy?"

"Who are you, Benedict Arnold?"

Louise rolled her eyes. "Don't overdo your parts, guys," she whispered.

Jasper hit the first ball just foul down the third baseline. However, he ran it out for a double.

"Very close," he shouted, "but fair."

"No way," said Amelia, who was pitching. "Foul by a mile."

Robby, who was playing third base, started making chicken noises.

"Ha, ha," said Jasper. "Fowl. I get it. But the ball was fair."

"Tell you what," said Amelia. "If you can get anyone to agree with you, we'll call it fair."

"Anyone?" said Jasper.

"Your choice."

"Deal." Jasper looked at his new apprentice sitting behind the backstop. "What do you think, Louise?"

Louise was expecting that. "I saw it the whole way," she said.

"And?" said Amelia.

"Looked fair to me."

"What?" Amelia threw down her glove in disgust. "Are you blind?"

Louise shrugged. "Just calling them as I see them."

"Next batter," said Jasper from second base.

Amelia picked up her glove. She got the next two batters out, but Jasper scored on a single to right field, putting his team ahead when the bell rang.

At lunch Louise followed Jasper around with a pile of napkins. Whenever Jasper finished eating something, he put out his hand, and Louise gave him a napkin. No fuss, no muss. When Jasper was done with each napkin, he crumpled it into a ball and dropped it into Louise's waiting hands.

After school Jasper stopped Alex and Emily on their way home. Louise stood at his side.

"I need to make a phone call," said Jasper. "Either of you have a quarter?"

"Not me," said Emily. "I'm saving up for your birthday present."

"Very thoughtful," said Jasper. "What about you, Alex?"

Alex hesitated. "Sorry," he blurted out.

"Oh, really?" said Jasper. "Why am I not convinced?"

He grabbed Alex's arm, dislodging his drawing pad and spilling markers from his pocket. A few coins fell out as well.

"Look what we have here. Found money.

Found by me, that is. You didn't even know you had it." He grinned. "Now you don't."

"Let me get that for you, Boss," said Louise.

She bent down and picked up the change.

"Boss?" said Alex.

"Louise works for me," Jasper explained.

Emily looked shocked. "You've gone over to the enemy."

"Not at all, Em," said Louise. "It's just a good career move."

"I never pictured you like that, Louise," said Alex.

"Well, start picturing," said Jasper. "Louise has become my apprentice. Any objections?"

"I think you deserve each other," said Emily.

Jasper laughed. "I can live with that. Now beat it."

Alex retrieved his pad and markers. Then he and Emily took off.

"This is working well," said Jasper.

Louise smiled. "I'm glad you're pleased."

"I'm more than pleased," said Jasper. "I can't wait until tomorrow."

"Me neither," said Louise. "This is only the beginning."

CHAPTER 8

The next morning Louise met Jasper in the playground before school. She handed him a piece of paper.

"What's this?" Jasper asked.

"The teams for today's baseball game at recess."

Jasper's eyes opened wide. "You made them up in advance. Let me see." He looked at the team rosters. "Wow! This way I'll win for sure."

"Of course. Who wants to wait around while Megan figures everything out? Speaking of Megan, look who's coming."

Megan had just appeared around the corner

of the building. She stopped short, though, when she saw Louise standing with Jasper. Then she turned and went back the other way.

"Not even a hello," said Jasper. "Some people are so rude."

"She certainly didn't look very happy."

"I bet she'll look even less happy later."

"There's a 99% chance of that."

Jasper laughed.

Louise was right. When Megan heard about the prepicked teams at recess, she was not pleased. "The odds of us winning—"she paused, "are not worth measuring."

Nevertheless, the game went on. As Megan had predicted, her team was trounced. Jasper's team scored so often that even he stopped keeping track after the first 23 runs.

When it was time for lunch, Jasper rushed to the cafeteria. All that running around had made him very hungry.

"I'm starved," he said. "Let's get started."

"Wait a minute, Boss," said Louise. "You don't have to rush around picking things at random."

"I don't?"

Louise consulted her notebook. "I've checked the lunches in advance."

"You have?"

She nodded. "Here are the top choices. Brendan's got a piece of his brother's birthday cake. Alyssa has fruit pastries from a party her parents had. And Elizabeth has a fancy deli sandwich."

"Does it—"

"Don't worry," she said, "I've already checked it for pickles."

Jasper was impressed. "That's very good, Louise."

"Thank you. But let's not waste time talking. Your lunch is waiting."

Jasper stuffed himself that day. It was all so easy and all so delicious. He didn't even have to move. Louise brought everything to his table.

"I'll bet even the pharaohs never ate this good," he declared.

That afternoon Jasper burped twice during math. But nobody dared to laugh.

The next day went just as smoothly. By the end of the week Jasper had gained three pounds.

On Monday Jasper arrived at school early. Louise had promised to create a new record-keeping system over the weekend. Jasper was looking forward to hearing about it.

Louise was waiting for him.

"I've been going over the records," she

said. "Efficiency is way up. For every cupcake that you ate before, you are now eating a cupcake and a half."

Jasper patted his stomach. "Sounds great to me," he said.

"But there's still room for growth," said Louise.

"Room for more cupcakes, you mean?"

"Exactly."

Jasper scratched his head. "So what do we do?"

Louise picked her words carefully. "Remember what it was like when you were on your own? Well, even the two of us have limits. What we need is another apprentice."

"Another?" Jasper stopped to think it over. Louise had certainly turned out to be a big help. Having another apprentice would be even better. "You know," he said, "I'll bet I'd be the only person in the state with two apprentices."

"Definitely," said Louise.

"But who should it be?"

"I was thinking that as things get more complicated, we should have someone who's good with numbers."

"You can't mean Megan?" Jasper laughed. "There's a 100% chance she hates me."

Louise shook her head. "Don't be so sure. You know how much Megan likes mathematical challenges. I'm sure she's never had the chance to be involved with an organization like yours."

Jasper hadn't thought of that.

"Still, what if she turns us down? That would look bad."

"The odds are in our favor."

Jasper nodded. Megan could crunch numbers while he crunched everyone else. "All right," he said.

Before the day was over, Megan had become Jasper's second apprentice. Louise explained to him that while it had taken a lot of convincing, the lure of so much computing was too much for Megan to resist.

"Louise, I have only one thing to say," Jasper told her upon hearing the news.

"What's that?"

"Keep up the good work."

"Oh, I will," said Louise. "You can depend on it."

CHAPTER 9

Together, Louise and Megan treated Jasper like royalty. They laughed at his jokes before he had the chance. They read the newspaper comics aloud to him. They even entered his name in contests on the back of cereal boxes.

Jasper was delighted.

A week later he saw a line of classmates waiting on the playground after school. Each of them was holding some books and papers. At the head of the line Louise and Megan were busy taking notes.

"What's going on?" Jasper asked.

"We're picking people to help you with your homework," Louise explained.

"But people are helping me already," Jasper pointed out.

"Yes, but you're just using whoever's around."

"With that method," said Megan, "there's a 37% chance of getting inefficient help. We want to do better."

Jasper nodded. "I see. It's kind of like the lunches."

"Exactly," said Louise.

This was all very well, but it still left Jasper with one question. "But, um, why is everyone so eager to cooperate? I mean, I haven't even threatened them."

"Megan was very convincing," Louise explained.

Jasper turned to Megan. "What did you say?"

"I pointed out that one way or another they would all be helping you in time. Which did they prefer—helping in a subject they liked or just taking their chances with whatever came up?"

"And that did it?"

"I crunched the numbers for them." Megan grinned. "The odds were very persuasive."

"Uh-huh."

"We do have a new idea, though," said Louise.

Jasper blinked. "Again?"

"Oh, yes. We think you could use the playground better."

"What do you mean?"

"Well, you know how crowded it gets at recess. Sometimes you might not get to use a swing right away because somebody else is on it."

"I hate that," said Jasper.

"We know you could force people off," said Megan, "but that would take extra effort on your part. Instead we thought we could save you a place at each piece of equipment."

"Makes sense," said Jasper.

"However," said Louise, "there's too much stuff for me and Megan to do already." She hesitated. "But if we had three more apprentices, there would be no problem."

Jasper nodded. "I see what you mean." The more he thought about this playground idea, the more he liked it. Besides, he would be the only kid in the country with five apprentices.

"Pick them out," he said grandly. "I know you can handle it."

That afternoon the three new apprentices—Alex, Dan, and Veronica—started their new jobs on the playground. As Jasper made his rounds, he always found a space open for him.

This is the life, he thought.

A week later Louise met again with Jasper. She took out a computerized chart and laid it on the grass. The graph was climbing sharply.

"As you can see," said Louise, "things are going very well."

Jasper grinned. He saw himself standing at the head of a mighty empire—JASPER, Inc.

Louise yawned.

"You look tired," said Jasper.

She smiled sleepily. "I was up pretty late preparing all this. There's a lot to keep track of these days."

Jasper frowned. Louise was a crucial part of his organization. If she was tired, she might start making mistakes.

"Would it help to get some more apprentices?" he asked.

Louise's eyes brightened. "What a good idea! I never would have thought of that. No wonder you're such a success."

Jasper beamed. He would be the only person in the world with so many apprentices.

"Get anyone you want," he said. "No need to bother me with details."

Suddenly Louise looked very much awake. "Whatever you say, Boss."

Jasper went back to thinking about his empire. Maybe he could get a penthouse with a basketball court and a pool. And a pinball machine in every room. A private jet would be nice too. He could travel to every state, eating a different flavor of ice cream in each one. He could even go to Italy for pizza and maybe inspect the spaghetti crops he had always wondered about.

This was going to be great.

CHAPTER 10

As Jasper had ordered, more and more apprentices were signed up. It was like having his own private army. Jasper loved it. The pharaoh Cheops must have felt the same way watching his pyramid get built.

There was only one small cloud on Jasper's horizon.

"We need to talk," he said to Louise at lunch.

She put down her tuna sandwich and took a sip of chocolate milk. "What's up?" she asked.

"I'm starving, that's what's up."

"I know we had lunch put aside for you.

Am I right, Megan?"

Megan checked her notes. "Yes. You had a choice of low-fat egg salad or peanut butter with mint jelly. For dessert there was orange Jell-O with marshmallows, or mushy apples." She looked up. "Did somebody take them?"

"No," said Jasper, "nobody took them. They're still here. Who would steal food like that?"

"Well," said Louise. "I'm just relieved. Aren't you relieved, Megan?"

"Absolutely."

Jasper grunted. "I'm glad we're all *relieved*. But there's still a problem."

"What is it?" Louise asked.

"The problem," said Jasper, gritting his teeth, "is that those are terrible choices."

"They are somewhat limited," Louise admitted. "But I'm not surprised. You have to expect this."

"I do?" Jasper didn't understand. "Why?"

"Because now you have so many apprentices."

"What difference does that make?"

"Well, they're all part of your team."

"And?"

"Naturally you're not taking any food from them."

Jasper frowned. "I'm not? How come?"

"Gee, Jasper, they work for you. You want them to do a good job, right? They can't do that on empty stomachs."

"I guess not." Still, there was something about this that bothered him.

The next Friday Louise and Jasper sat down for another update. Jasper was looking forward to it. Among Louise's other duties, she had collected gifts for him from different members of the class. Every week there had been a nice assortment of balls, kites, books, and action figures.

"So what did I get this week?" he asked.

Louise looked nervous. She fiddled with her pencil. "Collections are down, I'm afraid."

"Down?" Jasper didn't like the sound of that. "What does *down* mean?"

"Smaller. Shrinking. Getting—"

"Meaning?"

Louise took three baseball cards out of her pocket. Their corners looked chewed, like a dog had been playing with them.

"I know these look a little used. But actually most of the facts are quite readable. See? If you—"

"That's it?" Jasper thundered. "That's all you have for me! How can this be?"

"Well, nobody who works for you is giving you gifts. That wouldn't be appropriate."

"What about the rest?"

Louise paused. "There really is no rest.

At this point everyone is one of your apprentices."

Jasper gaped at her. "Everyone?"

Louise nodded. "It's incredible, isn't it? You've really built quite an empire. You probably have more apprentices than anyone in the galaxy. The universe, even."

"B-but . . . " Jasper sputtered. He pounded his fist into the ground. "Don't you see there's something wrong here? I'm not taking food from apprentices." He grunted. "I'm not getting gifts from apprentices." He grunted again. "If everyone's an apprentice, there's no one left to boss around."

"Gee," said Louise. "I was only following *your* orders. I thought you wanted all this."

Jasper snorted. "I thought I did too. But now I *unwant* it."

"What does that mean?"

"It means I want to arrange a meeting to fire everyone, even you, Louise. I want everything to go back to the way it was before."

"Okay," said Louise. "Tomorrow's Saturday, so we could do it in the morning. I'll make the calls tonight."

"You're taking this very well, Louise."

She shrugged. "I knew things would have to change at some point."

Jasper folded his arms. "Good," he said. "The sooner the better."

CHAPTER 11

Jasper was waiting on the playground as his apprentices began to assemble. He marched back and forth, wearing a rut in the grass. He knew what he had to say. This was no time to be soft. It was time to be tough.

Now that she had been fired, Louise sat on the grass with the others.

When everyone had arrived, he cleared his throat. "I have an announcement to make," he began. "I know you've all been working hard. I appreciate it, but that doesn't matter now. I've decided to make some changes."

"What kind of changes?" asked Emily.

"I'm getting to that," said Jasper. "There

are too many of you. Too many apprentices. So I'm dismissing you all." He folded his arms. "I've already fired Louise."

Everyone gasped.

"The rest of you I'm firing now. I want things to go back to the way they used to be."

Louise stood up. She looked at her classmates and then at Jasper.

"That may not be possible."

"What?" fumed Jasper. "It's possible if I say it's possible. Don't forget who's in charge here."

"Oh, I haven't forgotten," said Louise. "You can be sure of that. And you're right about one thing. It is *definitely* time for a change."

Everyone stood up. They circled Jasper. All of a sudden nobody looked very friendly.

"We're not going back," said Louise. "We're going forward. We're not going to let you bully us anymore."

"Oh?" Jasper frowned. "And who's going to stop me?"

"I am," said Emily.

"Me too," said Megan.

"Let me draw you a picture," Alex put in.

The others crowded around.

Jasper looked at their faces. Until that moment he had not noticed how big his apprentices had been getting. Some were tall enough to look him right in the eye. Others had muscles he was now seeing for the first time.

"I can still take any of you alone in a fight."

"Maybe," said Louise, "but nobody is alone here. We've learned to work together." She smiled. "Under your leadership, of course."

"I might still take you on."

Megan cleared her throat. "The odds of your winning such an encounter are barely 3%."

Jasper paused. "That's all?"

She nodded.

Jasper swallowed nervously. "All right, all right," he said. "I get the message. Never

mind the changes. You can all remain my apprentices."

"While you stay in charge of recess?"

"Yes."

"And eat our lunches?"

"And get your homework done?"

"Well, yes."

Everybody laughed. The sound sent a chill through Jasper.

"No," said Louise, "I think we've done all that long enough."

Jasper gulped. "Well, what's going to happen then?"

Now Louise was the one folding her arms. "Quite a lot," she said.

CHAPTER 12

The party was going very well. Jasper had explained to his parents that he wanted to celebrate the end of the Ancient Egypt unit by inviting the class over. His parents were happy to agree because, up to that point, Jasper rarely brought any friends home from school.

The real reason for the party was a little different. While surrounded by his classmates, Jasper had been given a choice. If he wished, he could become the class apprentice and serve everyone else for the rest of the year.

Jasper had shuddered at the thought.

Or he could throw a big party to make up

for all the trouble he'd caused.

It had not been hard for Jasper to decide.

His house was decorated for the event with hieroglyphic posters on the walls and refreshments piled into little pyramids. Many of the kids had come in costume, balancing Egyptian headpieces and wearing cardboard jewelry.

Louise was wearing a black wig for the event. It made her look more like Cleopatra, she thought.

Jasper was being a good host, moving throughout the room, reminding everyone to eat and drink.

"Relax, Jasper," said Louise. "You did a great job. It's a wonderful party."

"You're sure? I didn't want to take any chances." The idea of spending months and months as the class apprentice still made him nervous.

"I think you're safe."

Emily wandered over. "Hi, Louise. Good going, Jasper." She took a close look at his

outfit. "I see you're dressed like a pharaoh."

Jasper grinned. "A guy can dream, can't he?"

"A guy could have a pyramid dropped on his head too," Emily pointed out.

Jasper sighed. "I'll keep that in mind."

Louise just laughed.

She was still smiling that night, lying in bed with a book open on her lap. She was supposed to be reading, but she wasn't. Mostly she was thinking about the party.

Louise's parents poked their heads in the doorway. "Lights out in five minutes," said her father. "I gather you enjoyed your party."

Louise nodded. "I'll say."

"Good."

"Oh, Louise," her mother added. "I understand you helped Lionel put a coat of arms on his shield."

"He told you, huh?"

"He sure did. He also said it took a really long time and that you didn't yell at him once." Her mother smiled. "It's good to see you getting along so well with your brother."

Louise, of course, remembered that it was Lionel who had first mentioned the knight's apprentice.

"All things considered," she said, "I figured I owed him one."